MAC'S SPORTS REPORT

SIDELINE PRESSURE

Book design by Jake Nordby
Illustrations by Simon Rumble

Published in the United States by Jolly Fish Press, an imprint of North Star Editions, Inc.

First Edition
First Printing, 2018

Library of Congress Cataloging-in-Publication Data (pending)
978-1-63163-236-5 (paperback)
978-1-63163-235-8 (hardcover)

Jolly Fish Press
North Star Editions, Inc.
2297 Waters Drive
Mendota Heights, MN 55120
www.jollyfishpress.com

Printed in the United States of America

MAC'S SPORTS REPORT

SIDELINE PRESSURE

BY KYLE JACKSON

ILLUSTRATED BY SIMON RUMBLE

PREDATORS POUNCE IN SECOND HALF DESPITE DISRUPTIVE FAN

by Mac McKenzie

After a slow shooting start, Coyote Canyon Middle's boys' basketball team (8–2) was finally able to pry the lid off the basket in the second half. They made 8 of their final 17 shots from beyond the arc. For much of the first half, the game appeared to be a barn burner. But in the end, South Valley Charter (4–7) didn't have the firepower to keep up. The Predators handed South Valley its third loss in a row.

This win was an all-around team effort for the Predators. Four of the five starters reached double figures. The only Predator who couldn't buy a bucket was Drew Borders. Usually the squad's resident sharpshooter, Borders couldn't get the rim in his crosshairs tonight.

"Drew just had one of those nights," Coach Miller said with a shrug. "All good shooters have them. I'm confident he can work through it. The important thing is he was still there to cheer on his teammates."

Unfortunately, one of the fans in attendance didn't brush off Borders' bricks so easily. This fan spent much of the game loudly giving the player shooting tips. When Borders passed up an open look in the second half, the fan gave him an especially hard time.

Coach Miller finally told the fan to quiet down.

Once the rest of the Predators got hot, this tense moment between coach and fan was mostly forgotten. Winning, as they say, fixes everything. And the Predators have won four in a row and seven of their last nine.

CHAPTER 1

Stewart "Mac" McKenzie stares at his laptop. As THE sportswriter for *The Coyote Courier*, his middle school's online newspaper, Mac is in charge of reporting on all the biggest games.

As usual, he's working on a deadline. And he's running out of time.

Mac knows he should submit the story and be done with it. The diehard sports fans in his school probably expected the game summary hours ago. Besides, Mac's only in eighth grade. There's math and science and social studies and English homework to do.

But he keeps staring at his laptop. Often, Mac writes summaries of the game while it's still going on. He usually hits "Submit" as the final buzzer sounds.

But not this time. This time, he kept punching the keys of his laptop as the gym emptied out. He didn't realize how much time had passed until he saw his mom standing in front of him, her hands on her hips. Without a word, she grabbed his laptop and shoved it into his backpack, which was hanging off the back of his chair, while Mac wheeled himself out the door. In the car, she'd pretended to be upset. After all, she told him, she'd had a long day at the emergency room (she's a nurse), and she'd been waiting in the car for twenty minutes. With his dad and older sister out of town visiting colleges, and with the baby being only eight months old, she couldn't afford to wait around. But they both knew she liked how seriously he took his job. He never wanted to submit a sports story unfinished.

And this story? It's definitely unfinished.

Which is why he's been staring at it ever since they got home. It's now 11:34 p.m. and all the lights are turned off in the house—but here he is, on the living room couch, looking desperately at the glowing screen of his laptop.

Sure, the game recap already includes most of the basics—who won, who played well, a standard quote from Coach Miller. And frankly, that should be enough. In fact, it should be *more* than enough. The Predators' opponent wasn't good enough to get even this much coverage. All Mac really needs to write is "Our team beat a lousy team. The end." If the diehards want more info, they can check the box score.

Then again, the Predators' victory isn't the real story.

The *real* story is the unnamed fan who kept disrupting the game.

He might be unnamed in Mac's game summary, but he most definitely has a name in real life.

Larry Borders—renowned attorney-at-law. And Drew Borders' father.

The reason Mac hasn't included Larry's name is— well, he isn't exactly sure. Mac's a sportswriter, for one thing—not a gossip columnist. It isn't his job to report on stuff that happens outside the lines. Plus, he doesn't want to embarrass Drew by publishing his dad's behavior for all to read.

And his dad's behavior was definitely embarrassing. "Follow through!" he yelled at his son, over and over. He also bellowed to Drew to "Get your feet set!" and "Keep your elbow out front!" The rest of the fans—both parents and students—had been sitting in the bleachers across the court. But Drew's dad had gotten so worked up he started pacing the sidelines. When Drew tried to ignore him, his dad said, "Are you listening to me?"

Maybe this *was* a sports story. It sure seemed to affect the game. When his dad started hollering again, Drew looked downward toward the hardwood and nodded his head. "If you're listening," his dad said, "then why aren't you doing it?"

At the end of the first half, Larry Borders approached

his son and grabbed his shoulder. He barked more shooting tips. Drew finally shrugged him off and said, "I have to go listen to Coach's halftime talk."

Come to think of it, it wasn't just Drew who was affected. The whole team played stiffly right up until Coach finally confronted Mr. Borders.

Without even realizing it, Mac starts to type up the altercation.

Noah Crowder skipped a pass cross court and Borders found himself alone. Usually, Borders is deadly from there. On the season he's shooting over 45 percent from that very corner. But this time—after a game of loud clanks and even louder comments from his father—Borders flinched. He hesitated. Not for long, but long enough for the South Valley defender to close out. Another defender followed. One second Borders had an uncontested look; the next, he was trapped. Coach Miller called a timeout, and the players hustled to their benches.

The only player who didn't move was Borders. He couldn't. Not with the vice grip his father had on his shoulder.

"Great shooters shoot!" his dad told him. "No matter

how many times a great shooter misses, he always knows the next shot is going in! You've got to be psychologically tougher than this, Drew. You hear me? I said, *do you hear me*?"

"That's enough."

It was Coach Miller who said it. From across the court.

"Did you hear me, Larry?" It was Coach Miller again. "Either put a cork in it or leave."

Mr. Borders *had* heard him. That was clear. The two of them stared each other down from opposite sides of the court. Mr. Borders swiped at his mustache and opened his mouth to say something, but then thought better of it.

He took Coach Miller up on his second offer. In other words, he left.

WAAAAAAAAA!

The sound jars Mac out of the story.

WAAAAAAA!

It's his eight-month-old baby sister, Nora.

This isn't the first time over the last several months that he's woken her. He sometimes gets so focused on what he's typing that he starts to punch the computer keys instead of simply tap them. That's all it takes these days to wake her. Other things that wrench her out of sleep: a creak from the wooden floor; a flushing toilet. Sometimes, it seems, just breathing or blinking are too loud.

In any case, the family rule is *Whoever wakes her, puts her back to sleep.*

Mac decides then and there that it's not worth making a big story out of Drew's dad's big mouth. He highlights the words he just typed and deletes them.

WAAAAAAAAA!

Mac lifts himself from the couch and into his chair and heads for Nora's bedroom.

Besides, he thinks, *judging by the way Larry Borders stormed out of the gymnasium, there will be other chances to write about his behavior.*

CHAPTER 2

"Did you talk to Borders yet?" someone asks Mac.

Mac doesn't have time to point out he just got to school.

"Dude, Drew's looking for you," someone else says. "He read your article about him."

Mac turns the corner, entering another hallway.

"Mac, Drew is—"

"Looking for me," Mac says. "So I've heard."

"He seemed pretty upset."

"Why?" Mac says. After all, Mac had decided *not* to include much about Drew or his dad in the article. If anything, shouldn't Drew be relieved?

"I'm sure he'll tell you when he finds you," someone says.

The rest of the day is the same. Every time he rolls through the halls, Mac is asked about Drew. Have you seen him? Has he seen you? He's looking for you, and he doesn't look too happy.

Mac just shrugs. When you're a sportswriter, unhappy athletes go with the territory. If everyone's always happy with you, you're not doing your job. That's what Mac tells himself, and he mostly believes it. But there's also a part of him that *isn't* okay making people angry. Try as he might, he can't help caring what other people think of him. Besides, what if someone got *really* angry with something he wrote? What would they do?

As Mac weaves his way through the crowded hallways, he half-expects to see Drew at any moment making a beeline for him, steam coming out of his ears.

Honestly, the day would be less nerve-wracking if Mac had classes with Drew. He has in the past. But Coyote Canyon is a big school, and this year Mac and Drew's schedules don't overlap. They don't even have lunch together.

Speaking of lunch, Mac is hoping it will be a nice break from classes and worrying about Drew.

"What's Drew's problem?" asks Samira.

She walks to their usual table, holding two lunch trays—one in each hand.

"Forget it," Mac says.

"Did you hear he's looking for you?"

"It's fine, Samira."

She's Mac's best friend. If anything, she's even more of a sports nut than he is.

Samira sets the trays on the table—one for him, one for her—and slides onto the seat across from Mac.

"Seriously—has he seen his plus-minus for the game?" she asks, taking a bite of her apple. Like most school apples, this one's overly red and mushy. Samira makes a face as she chews. "Were you supposed to write that he played well?"

Samira keeps track of tons of stats—points and assists and rebounds, of course, but also shooting percentages, how many points a player gave up on the defensive end, their plus-minus score, etc.

"I don't think it's his plus-minus that he's worried about," Mac says, dipping his french fry in ketchup. "He might be mad that I wrote about his dad."

"You didn't mention his dad. I mean, not technically."

"Not sure a technicality is going to make him feel any better."

Samira thinks about this while eyeing the apple again. She cautiously takes another bite, as if caution will change the way the apple tastes. It doesn't. Samira tosses the apple onto her tray. The two friends watch the apple wobble and fall to its side.

"If I were him, I'd be more worried about my plus-minus," Samira says.

"That's because you're weird."

"You would too," Samira says.

"That's because I'm weird too."

For the remainder of lunch they eat and talk about

sports: man-to-man defense vs. zone, the designated hitter rule, how and when instant replay should be used.

It isn't until they're emptying what's left of their trays into the garbage that Samira brings up Drew again.

"Want me to help you tell Drew his priorities are all mixed up?"

Because they're best friends, Mac knows she actually means: *Want me to be there as backup when Drew finds you?*

"I'm good," he says.

"You sure?"

Mac shrugs. "No, but I'm sure I don't want a bodyguard."

"I didn't mean that you *needed* one. I just—"

"No worries, Samira," Mac interrupts. "Thanks for offering. Really."

They leave the cafeteria together, this time talking about whether face guarding in football should be considered pass interference.

Amazingly, despite continuing to hear about Drew all day, Mac never sees him. No text or anything, which is probably for the best.

Maybe Drew will calm down by tomorrow, he thinks.

Once almost all the students have left the building, and Mac's sure no one will hear him, he breathes a sigh of relief.

He heads for the journalism classroom—or, as he likes to call it, the *bullpen*. It's usually empty right after school. Mac likes to study the giant calendar he has tacked to the wall. It highlights every sports team's schedule. It's in the bullpen where Mac usually decides which sport or game to cover next.

"Hey."

There, sitting at Mac's desk, is Drew Borders.

Mac hesitates in the doorway, considers leaving, but then grabs the wheels on either side of his chair and continues toward his desk.

The last thing you want to do as a reporter is back away from a story.

"I need to talk to you," Drew says.

"Aren't you supposed to be at practice?" Mac asks.

Mac isn't exactly sure of the basketball practice schedule, but Drew's in his practice gear. He's wearing a reversible jersey that's crunchy from dried old sweat. His sneakers are untied.

"I have a couple minutes," Drew says. He stands up. Mac had forgotten how tall he is. He plays guard, after all. Drew crosses his muscular arms. It occurs to Mac that those arms could knock him to the floor with one swipe.

"The article," Drew says.

"Look, Drew, I'm sorry if you didn't like what I wrote, but—"

"Like it," Drew interrupts. "I loved it."

"What?" Mac thinks he must have heard him incorrectly.

Mac was prepared to defend the article. He was ready to say he was just doing his job. If need be, he was even willing to explain that the article could have been a whole lot worse. What he wasn't prepared for is a compliment.

"I said you shot bricks," he reminds Drew.

"I *did* shoot bricks," Drew says.

"I talked about your dad," Mac reminds him. "I didn't say his name, but anyone who was there would know who I was talking about."

"That's more than fair, given what happened."

Mac can't think of anything else to say except, "Thanks for understanding."

"No problem, Mac."

Neither of them say anything for a few moments.

"I guess I'm the one who doesn't understand," Mac

offers. "If you aren't upset about the article, why did you come see me?"

Drew scratches his elbows as he thinks about Mac's question. "To say thank you," Drew says.

"For what?"

"For getting my dad off my back."

"How did my article do that?" Mac can't hide the surprise from his voice.

"My dad hates being a laughing stock."

"I wasn't trying to make him a laughing stock," Mac says.

Drew shakes his head. "He did a good job of that all on his own."

More silence.

"And my article got your dad off your back?" Mac asks.

"I hope so. I know he read it last night."

"Really? I didn't submit this one until pretty late."

"He reads all your articles. He's like your biggest fan."

Mac smiles at the compliment. "Why? I mean, I'm a middle schooler, writing about a middle school basketball team."

"That's what I told him. He said that if I wanted people to take me seriously, I needed to take my life seriously." Drew rolls his eyes.

"What does that mean?"

"I didn't ask. He can be pretty intense. Maybe your article will be a wake-up call, you know? Maybe he'll tone it down a little."

"Yeah. Maybe," Mac says. *But then again*, he thinks, *people who take themselves seriously have a tendency to take themselves* too *seriously. And people who take themselves too seriously aren't very good at toning it down.*

"I better get to practice," Drew says, patting Mac's shoulder. "See you at the game tomorrow."

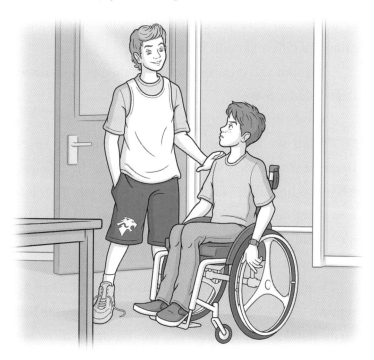

CHAPTER 3

Mac shows up for the game during warm ups. He positions his chair in his usual place: the corner of the gymnasium, by one of the exits. It's not an ideal place to watch a game, but it has its advantages. People can't bug him there. They can't look over his shoulder at what he's writing, or block his view by standing up to cheer. Thanks to the doors next to him, he can leave quickly if necessary to cover another game at a different court or field.

That spot also ensures that Mac is the first one to see Drew's dad arrive.

Everybody else hears him before they see him.

"What are you doing rebounding your own shot, Drew?" Larry Borders says. He strides along the sideline, talking as he walks. "That's a non-starter's job. Your job is to shoot—as many shots as possible. That way you'll be more ready for the game than last time."

Drew looks at him, stunned.

"Well don't just stand there, Son," Larry says. Then he repeats: "Shots. You need to make some shots. See the ball go in. Build up the confidence." Mr. Borders' voice isn't loud—he's having a conversation with his son—but it's loud enough. He's the only parent talking.

"I can rebound for you," Jeremy Backstrom says. Jeremy is indeed a non-starter, but more importantly, he's a nice kid. Mac's pretty sure Jeremy's just trying to help Drew out of an awkward situation. "Go ahead, Drew. I'll keep passing you the ball back when you shoot."

As Drew shoots, his father tells him to keep moving around and gives more advice about his form.

Yesterday, Drew had been optimistic that his dad would be less intense at his next game. But if anything, it's the opposite. Mac's never seen Mr. Borders begin his sideline antics before the game has even started.

The buzzer sounds. The players hustle to their bench for some last-minute conversation with their coaches.

The buzzer sounds again. Game time.

The starters shuffle back to the court, tucking in their jerseys and pointing to who they're going to guard.

One problem: for the first time all season, Drew's not in the starting lineup. Mac spots him sitting at the end of the bench, shoulders hunched.

Drew's dad is talking to some other parents and hasn't noticed yet. But he will soon enough.

This could get interesting, Mac thinks.

PREDATORS LOSE WITHOUT PUTTING UP MUCH OF A FIGHT

by Mac McKenzie

For the second game in a row, Coyote Canyon Middle's boys' basketball team (8–3) got off to a lackluster start. This time, they never recovered. But to give credit where credit's due, their opponent, the East River Raiders (6–6), made tough shots from beginning to end. They never trailed.

East River guard Nick Delgado was particularly impressive, making his first five shots, including a long heave at the end of the first half. Delgado finished with 17 points, a season high.

While the Raiders were draining deep shots, the Predators missed from everywhere, including right under the basket. Despite a noticeable height advantage, the Predators' frontcourt players couldn't convert a number of point-blank put-backs.

Coyote Canyon will have a long weekend to get the loss out of their system. Then they'll hit the road next week against their archrivals, the Middlefield Lions, who at 7–4 are in second place and closing in fast.

CHAPTER 4

"Shhhhh," Mac says.

He's done it again. His furious typing woke up Nora. He swings open the guardrail on the crib, scoops up his crying sister, and sways back and forth.

WAAAAAAAAA!

Cradling her in one arm, he backs up his chair with the other. By now, the two of them have a routine. Mac has to do most of the heavy lifting. (Literally. At close to twenty pounds, Nora seems to be getting heavier every night.) It's his job to carry Nora, to rock her, to make endless loops through the dining room, the kitchen, the living room. It's her job to fall back asleep. The only way the routine varies is how many loops it takes before Nora drifts off.

They've only done a couple loops before she is sleeping.

But Mac doesn't notice. He's too riled up about the game—and about his game recap.

He once again decided, at the last second, to highlight and delete half his article before sending it in. This time he didn't include anything about Drew's father.

Did he make the right call?

He pivots his chair through the kitchen doorway and into the dining room, his baby sister breathing peacefully.

If anything, Drew's dad had been worse than last time.

When he saw Drew on the bench, he hollered across the bench . . . at the coach.

"Are you serious, Coach?" he said. "Benching my kid because you're mad at me for doing *your* job? Is that what this is?"

He hadn't stopped there.

A few minutes later, when Drew was still on the bench, Larry Borders raised his voice again: "You're a class act, Coach. Taking out your frustration with me on your own team."

It didn't help that the Predators got off to such a slow start.

"You're willing to lose just to . . . what? Shut me up? Put me in my place? News flash, Coach: this isn't about you or me. It's about the team. It's about the kids."

It was strange. As far as Mac could see, Larry Borders was the one who was making the game about himself. But he was making it sound like Coach Miller was the problem.

And the longer Drew stayed on the bench as the

Predators fell farther and farther behind, the longer it seemed like Larry Borders had a point.

Mac found himself wanting Coach to do something. Put Drew in. Kick Larry out. Something. *Anything*.

Instead, he ignored Larry completely. And it sure seemed as though he ignored Drew too.

Yes, Larry was being totally inappropriate. But from a purely basketball standpoint, Mac had to admit that he was sort of right. If there was ever a time to have your best shooter on the court, it was when you were trying to make a comeback.

The comeback never happened. And Drew's dad never stopped talking. He'd pipe down for a few minutes, but sooner or later he'd yell at the coach again.

"Bravo, Coach," he said at the end of the game. "You win. Your team loses, but you win."

Drew, for his part, had hardly moved a muscle. He sat at the end of the bench the whole game. He was still sitting there as the two teams lined up and shook hands.

Mac included all of this in the recap. He asked why the other parents hadn't spoken up and put a stop to Larry's commentary. He admitted that he didn't know why, exactly, Drew hadn't played, but he kept the focus on Larry and his antics. Someone, he decided, needed to hold this man accountable, to suggest that he wasn't allowed to attend any more games—not until he could control himself. If neither the parents nor the coach would do this, he would.

When he finished, and Nora started crying, he realized he hadn't been writing a game recap so much as venting. He'd been editorializing rather than reporting.

He'd gotten so caught up in his anger that he'd forgotten to interview any of the players or coaches.

That's why he deleted all the stuff about Drew's dad.

It wasn't his role to get high and mighty—at least it wasn't supposed to be.

And yet, as he does one more loop with Nora sleeping on his lap, he can't help thinking that he hasn't done enough. It may not be his job to editorialize, but it's also not his job to edit.

He sets Nora gently into her crib, quietly closes the guardrail, and latches the bolt. He decides that tomorrow he'll interview Coach, Drew, maybe even a parent or two. He'll even interview Larry Borders.

Rather than avoid the story, he'll find people who are willing to tell their version of it.

CHAPTER 5

Mac gets to school early the next morning and makes his way down to the gym. Before he opens the gym doors he hears a basketball bouncing, just as he thought he would.

"Hey, Diego," he says, gliding toward the court.

Diego Lunez, a backup forward, nods his head at Mac but doesn't stop dribbling. He's actually got two basketballs, one for each hand. At first, he dribbles them simultaneously, both hitting the hardwood at the same time, then he changes the rhythm so they alternate, then he crosses the basketballs over, switching hands.

Diego has been doing this routine every day for almost a year. Soon he'll switch from dribbling to shooting. After a couple hundred shots, he'll run wind sprints. Mac knows all this because some mornings he joins Diego in these early-morning practices. He once told Mac that his goal is to become a starter. So far, that hasn't happened—but that hasn't stopped him from putting in extra work every morning. It also hasn't stopped him from being a great teammate. Mac often goes to Diego when he's looking for a positive quote about a specific player or the team in general.

Diego rolls one of the basketballs gently toward the wall and then stations himself five feet in front of the hoop. He'll stay there, Mac knows, until he's made ten shots in a row from that spot. Afterward, he'll find a different spot and make ten more.

Mac stations himself under the basket. Diego takes and makes a shot, and Mac catches the ball after it drops through the rim.

"Mind if I ask you a few questions about yesterday's game?" Mac asks, passing Diego the ball.

Diego doesn't respond, but that's normal. It usually takes him a while to warm up. Mac's learned that if he just keeps asking questions, pretty soon Diego can't help himself. He loves basketball too much to not want to talk about it.

"You played well," Mac says.

"Thanks," Diego says, taking another shot.

That's more like it, Mac thinks. Pretty soon, Mac guesses, Diego will be chatting away.

"Pretty weird, though," Mac says, passing Diego the ball again, "Coach Miller benching Drew like that. I mean, I know he didn't shoot very well last game, but—"

"That's between Coach and Drew," Diego says curtly.

It's not like Diego to interrupt a question. Or to sound so harsh.

He keeps his eyes on the rim as he takes another shot. It clanks off the rim. Mac knows he'll start his counting all over.

"I'm actually going to talk to Coach next," Mac says, chasing down the missed shot and chest passing it back to Diego. "I just figured I should get a player's response too."

"Drew's a player," Diego says. "Talk to him."

"So Coach didn't explain to the team why he was benching Drew?" Mac asks.

"It's Coach's decision who plays—not mine." Diego makes another shot.

"I know," Mac says. "But did he talk about the decision to the rest of the team?"

"Talk to Coach," Diego repeats.

"Did you agree with the benching?"

"It's not my job to agree or disagree," Diego says. "I just play when Coach asks me to."

"Did Coach tell you not to talk about this with me?" Mac asks, catching another make.

"You'll have to talk to Coach about that."

"So that's a yes then?" Mac says.

He stays there for several more minutes, waiting for Diego to talk.

But Diego makes his ten shots in silence and moves farther away to make ten more. Mac rebounds a few more makes and then gives up on getting any information.

"Coach?" Mac asks. "Got a second?"

Coach Miller's in his office with his feet on his desk and a book in his hands just inches from his face. The book's called *The Breaks of the Game*.

Coach must be pretty engrossed because he doesn't lower the book.

"Is that the Halberstam book?" Mac asks. "The one about the Portland Trail Blazers?"

Technically, these are real questions. One of Coach Miller's hands is covering the author's name. But Mac actually knows the answers to these questions. Yes, it's the Halberstam book. He knows because he's read it several times. The purpose of the questions is to get Coach's attention by making small talk.

It doesn't work.

Coach must not hear him because the book doesn't lower.

Mac decides to try knocking on the already open door. Still nothing. No wonder he's able to ignore Drew's dad throughout the game; the man appears to be deaf.

Mac knocks again—this time really banging on the door.

Finally, Coach takes his feet off his desk and sets the book down in front of him.

"McKenzie," he says to Mac.

"Hi, Coach. Wondering if I could ask a few questions about the game last night."

"Shoot."

"Thanks. My first question is—"

"No, I'm saying *shoot*. That's what we needed to do. Shoot. More and better."

By now, Mac is used to Coach doing stuff like this. Making jokes that might not be jokes. Trying to trip up his questions. Coach is notorious for being difficult to talk to, but Mac doesn't mind. It makes interviewing him a challenge—a challenge that Mac fully accepts. Especially since he's always believed that Coach isn't really as gruff as he pretends to be.

"That's actually what I was going to ask about," Mac says. "If you needed shooting, why not play your best shooter?"

The expression on Coach's face changes. It hardens or something. It's not as though Coach has ever been much of a smiler, but Mac has always seen some warmth in his eyes, even if no one else could. "There's a twinkle there," Mac had once told Samira. "What does a twinkle look like?" she'd asked. Mac hadn't known what to tell her. In any case, whatever twinkle he'd previously seen is gone now.

"It's my job as the coach to decide who plays when," Coach Miller says.

"I know," Mac says, telling himself not to back down or let his voice waver. "What I'm asking is *why* you made the decision to bench Drew. Was it because of Drew's dad?"

"As long as I'm the coach, I get to determine which five players to send out to the court."

"I know, Coach," Mac repeats, "but I was hoping you'd answer—"

Coach Miller interrupts Mac. "I did answer. Twice."

"That wasn't my question, though."

"Well, it was my answer. I get to do whatever I think is best for the team, McKenzie."

"I get that. But—"

"The interview's over," Coach Miller says.

He lifts his book in front of his face.

Mac turns for the door.

"Nice try with the Halberstam question, by the way."

Mac looks over his shoulder. "Coach?"

Coach Miller lowers the book and looks straight at Mac. "I don't buy for a second that a reporter as good as you hasn't read a classic like *The Breaks of the Game*. But good for you for trying to butter me up, McKenzie."

"I wasn't trying to butter you up, Coach. I was—"

"No offense taken, McKenzie. You were just trying to do your job. That's what I'm trying to do too."

Mac's not entirely sure why Coach has said these last few things, but he's pretty sure Coach was giving him a compliment. He's also pretty sure that the twinkle in Coach's eye has returned.

Coach Miller puts the book in front of his face before Mac can look too close and find out.

Next up, Mac decides, is to call Drew's dad. This is something he really doesn't want to do. Larry Borders has already made it abundantly clear how he feels about the situation. What's the point of interviewing someone when you, and everyone else, already know what he's going to say?

But to write a fair and balanced story, Mac realizes, he'll need to get quotes from all relevant parties. That obviously includes Larry Borders.

There are still ten minutes before school starts. Mac is at his desk in the bullpen. Parker Sanders, another reporter for the *Courier*, is a few desks away working on a story. Mac had tried to make small talk with Parker when Mac first arrived at the bullpen, but Parker hadn't heard him—which isn't surprising. Parker gets so focused on his work that you have to literally shake him to get his attention.

Mac turns his attention back to his own work. So far, he has struck out twice in his attempts to get interviews from people he actually wants to hear from. Now he's about to interview someone he has no interest in hearing from, and he's guessing that person will gladly answer his questions. After all, if there's one thing that Larry Borders clearly loves, it's the sound of his own voice. In fact, at the beginning of the season, when Mac passed out his phone number to the team (just in case there was ever anything sports-related they thought he should know), it was Drew's *dad* who called him. He wanted Mac to know, he said, that he'd be happy to offer game analysis and insight.

Mac has never taken Larry Borders up on this offer, and still doesn't want to.

Which is why, instead of calling Larry, Mac opens the voice recorder app on his cell phone. Usually this is something he does to get his thoughts in order, but today it has more to do with his desire to delay calling Drew's dad.

"Come to think of it," he says into the phone's recorder, "this whole situation isn't funny at all. It's irritating. And it's strange. Why were Diego and Coach Miller so unwilling to talk to me?"

He stops recording as he gives the situation more thought. Coach has never exactly loved answering questions, Mac thinks, but usually he at least provided standard clichés. *One game at a time, win with defense,* etc.

After one of the losses this year, Mac made the mistake of asking, "What do you need to do to make sure this loss doesn't become a losing streak?"

"Win," Coach had said.

But even if his answers were sometimes short and not all that helpful, Coach had never before today refused to even acknowledge Mac's questions. Diego had never stonewalled him before either. Opening the recorder app again, Mac says, "It's almost like they're protecting someone. But who?"

"Me."

Mac closes the recorder app once again. Drew is standing in the doorway of the bullpen.

Mac thinks of asking a follow-up question, but decides against it. His instincts tell him Drew is going to keep talking on his own.

He's in street clothes instead of his jersey: a hooded sweatshirt and jeans.

"Just talked with Coach," Drew says. "He told me you couldn't have gotten far."

Mac nods but doesn't interrupt. He watches Drew step into the bullpen and close the door behind him. Drew suddenly realizes they're not alone. He points to Parker.

"Maybe we can talk somewhere else?" he says to Mac.

Mac considers this. "Probably easier to have Parker leave." He tries calling his name a few times, but Parker stays hunched over his computer screen. Mac picks up a tennis ball from his desk. Throwing the ball against the wall sometimes helps him think. This time, instead of throwing the ball off the wall, he tosses it gently at Parker. The tennis ball bounces off Parker's head.

"What the . . . ?" Parker says.

"Sorry," Mac says. "Couldn't get your attention. Any chance we could have the room for a few minutes?"

Parker looks around the bullpen, sees Drew, and nods. "Just let me finish this sentence and save what I've got."

"Thanks," Mac says.

A few minutes later, after Parker's left the room, Mac says, "You came to tell me something?"

"I asked Coach to bench me," Drew says.

He's talking more quietly than normal, as if Parker or someone else might be listening from the hallway.

"You did?" Mac asks. "Why?"

"You saw him," Drew says.

"Your dad." This isn't a question so much as a statement.

Now it's Drew's turn to nod. "I can't do it anymore. Playing basketball used to be fun. Now it's just embarrassing."

Drew's eyes are watery, but Mac can't tell if he's crying or just angry.

"Why don't you quit?" Mac asks.

"Do you really think there's any chance my dad would let me do that?" Drew asks.

"What did he say when you told him?"

"Told him what?"

"That you asked to be benched?" Mac says.

"I didn't tell him." Drew looks sad. "I . . . can't."

For some reason, Mac has been slow to understand what was really going on. Maybe it's because he's spent the last few games feeling sorry for Drew, or because he's always thought of Drew as a decent enough guy. It's only registering now what Drew is saying.

"You let Coach take the heat for you?" Mac asks.

"No. I mean, yes. But Coach said it was okay." He puts his hands over his face, then combs his hands through his hair. "I know it's bad. But that's why I'm here. To clear everything up."

"You want me to write an article about it?" Mac says. "Why not just tell your dad yourself?"

Drew takes a deep breath. "I told you, I can't talk with him about this. I just . . . can't."

Mac doesn't get it. Whether Drew tells him in person

or Mac writes a story about it, Drew's dad is going to find out. Would it really be less upsetting for him to read about his son's decision than to hear about it from him directly?

Then again, Mac is a reporter—and this is some story.

He turns his phone to Drew to show him the voice recorder app. Then he turns the app on and says, "Whenever you're ready."

But Drew doesn't confess. He doesn't speak at all. Instead, he shakes his head and waves his arms.

Mac turns off the app.

"I'm not going on the record," Drew says.

"What do you mean?"

"I'm an anonymous source."

"What?" Mac isn't sure he understands what Drew is trying to accomplish.

"If I go on record, then Dad will know it was me. He'll know that I'm the source."

"That's how sources work," Mac says.

"Not anonymous ones."

"Sorry, Drew," Mac shakes his head. "We don't use anonymous sources at *The Coyote Courier*."

"Oh." Drew pulls on one end of his hoodie's drawstring, then wraps it around his finger until the tip goes white.

Mac's pretty sure that Drew is unaware of what he's doing. He's too deep in thought. "You can't or you won't?"

"We can't," Mac says. "It's against our editorial policy."

Drew winds and unwinds the drawstring around his finger. He does this at least three more times before the first-hour bell rings. "I better go," he says, and then turns to leave.

"Wait, Drew," Mac says.

"Yeah?" Drew's reaching for the door handle but stops.

"What are you going to do?" Mac asks him.

"I don't know," Drew says. "Keep riding the bench for now."

CHAPTER 6

Mac watches his teammate, Ty Warren, dribble the ball up the court.

28 seconds left in the game. 27 . . . 26 . . .

Be patient, he reminds himself.

21 . . . 20 . . .

His team, the Wizards on Wheels, is down a layup. For that reason, their opponent, Groveland District, is jamming the lane. Four of their five defenders have stationed their chairs in or near the lane.

17 . . . 16 . . .

The only defender who isn't clogging the lane is the one guarding Mac. By now, he's used to it. Teams almost always trail him everywhere he goes on the court. Usually, they double team him too.

But not this time.

Which is a mistake on their part.

11 . . . 10 . . .

Mac can't afford to wait any longer. He cuts straight across the top of the key, just close enough to the other

defenders and his own teammates that the guy guarding him gets caught up among the other chairs.

7 . . . 6 . . .

He turns his head to see Ty fake a pass to his right and then, with one hand, toss the ball toward Mac. The pass lands right in Mac's hands. Stopping on a dime, he takes one dribble while rotating his chair and then . . .

3 . . . 2 . . .

. . . Mac releases the ball with plenty of backspin. Everyone on the court swivels and cranes their necks to watch the basketball arc through the air.

Everyone, that is, except for Mac. He keeps his eyes fastened to the rim.

Though even that is unnecessary.

As soon as the ball left his hand, he knew it was going in.

The buzzer goes off at almost the same time the basketball goes through the hoop.

The ref puts his arms in the air to signal both a three-pointer and another Wizards win.

"You guys are shooting too many long two-point shots," Samira says. She helps herself to a slice of pizza.

That's what the three of them—Samira, Mac, and Ty—are doing: eating pizza. It's supposed to be celebratory pizza, but Samira isn't in the celebrating mood.

"You guys really put yourself behind the eight ball by taking stupid shots," she says.

"Are you serious?" Ty says. He goes to a different school than Mac and Samira; the Wizards are made up of students from three local middle schools. That means that, unlike Mac, Ty hasn't gotten used to Samira's constant game analysis. "My boy here nailed a *three-pointer* to win the game—what game were you even watching?"

He's pretending to be exasperated with her, but really he just likes egging her on. He dips a breadstick into some sauce.

"The game where you and your teammates shot—and made—nine shots within a foot of the arc. See? I made a chart." She pulls out a piece of paper from her pocket and unfolds it. The paper has a court drawn on it. Sure enough, Samira's kept track of every shot Mac and Ty's team took. "If you moved behind the line throughout the game you wouldn't have needed Mac to bail you out at the end."

"Bail us out?" Ty says. "Are you listening to this girl, Mac?"

Mac *is* listening, but just barely. He's deep in thought.

"Basketball's an escape, right?" Mac says.

"What?" Ty asks.

"Playing basketball," Mac continues. "It's my escape from real life. It's not that real life is bad, it's just that sometimes I need a break, you know? Basketball's my escape," he says again.

Ty and Samira look at each other, shrug.

"Everything okay, Mac?" Ty says.

"Huh?" Mac says. "Oh. Yeah. Everything's fine. I was just thinking how weird it would be to have to escape from something that's supposed to be an escape itself."

He knows he's being vague, but he can't tell them exactly what he's thinking about: Drew *asking* to be benched. After all, Drew didn't go on the record, so Mac has to pretend that the conversation he had with him yesterday in the bullpen never happened.

"Sure, Mac," Ty says. "I have no idea what you're talking about, but I can tell it's deep."

The three eat pizza together in silence for a while.

"Just so we're clear," Ty says to Samira, "I don't understand half the stuff that comes out of *your* mouth either. All those stats I've never heard of."

Samira pulls out her chart again and says, "It's really not that complicated . . ."

CHAPTER 7

On Monday, Coyote Canyon has a road game against Middlefield. Typically, Mac doesn't cover away games; there are enough sporting events at Coyote Canyon most days to keep him plenty busy.

But today he asks his mom for a ride.

"It's a big game," he explains to her. "First-place team against second."

This is true, but it's not the real reason he wants to cover the game. It occurred to him over the weekend that Middlefield isn't only away—it's hours away.

Which means that maybe Larry Borders won't show up. And if he doesn't show up, maybe Drew would agree to play.

In other words, Mac wants to go to the game mostly so he can see what happens next. Whatever it is, it's bound to be dramatic.

As it turns out, the game isn't actually very dramatic. Not after the first few minutes, anyway.

Larry is there, front and center, twenty minutes before game time.

Weirdly, though, Coyote Canyon isn't.

There is a running clock ticking away—17 minutes and 58 . . . 57 . . . 56 seconds until the game is supposed to start.

But the Predators are M.I.A.

They haven't been gone long enough for any real concern. Parents are just starting to take notice.

But Mac's pretty sure something is up. It's not like Coach Miller and his team to be even a second late. So Mac goes looking for them. He checks the locker room but they aren't there. He speeds through the halls, searching for another court—but all he finds are more hallways and classrooms and, on the very other end of the building, a pool. This pool has a locker room as well but it too is empty. Mac looks at the clock on his phone: only six minutes until game time.

Then he has a thought: has the bus even arrived? He hurries back across the building and out the doors to the parking lot. Sure enough, the bus is parked and empty, save for the driver, who is looking at his cell phone while blasting music from the bus's loudspeaker.

Mac is just about to give up when he hears a ball bouncing. The sound is faint—clearly from a long way away—but for a basketball writer and player like Mac, it's unmistakable. He wheels down the sidewalk and turns the corner at the end of the building, the bounces getting louder as he moves.

Finally, there are the Predators. They're going through their warm-up drills on the outside basketball court. At first, Mac has no idea what they're doing out here. The hoop they're shooting at is clearly not meant for official, organized basketball. There are actually two rims, fused together to prevent them from snapping when someone hangs from them. As any basketball player knows, though, fusing two rims together also makes it a lot harder to make shots. Basketballs don't just glance off two rims; they ricochet off them. Any shot that isn't a swish is a complete brick. The wind isn't helping the Predators' shots go in either.

And yet none of them seem to mind.

They're laughing with one another and taking turns shooting.

No one seems happier than Drew. The last few games he's been silent and sulky, but right now he's beaming.

"Game time is in less than a minute," Mac says to Coach Miller, who's standing at the edge of the court, looking at his gamebook.

Coach looks at his watch.

"Yikes," he says, fumbling for his whistle and finally blowing it.

"To the court, gentleman," Coach barks to his team. "We're running late."

The players hurriedly scramble off the court and run toward the school building.

Mac and Coach Miller are still back at the courts, watching the players rush across the parking lot.

"Can I ask you why you had them warm up out here?" Mac says. "Or are you just going to tell me that as the coach you can have them warm up wherever you want?"

Coach snorts. "Touché, McKenzie. I guess I just thought we needed a break from all the attention we've been getting lately during our pre-game warm up."

They both know Coach is talking about Larry Borders.

"He's in there," Mac says.

"I know it. That's why we were out here. To give us a chance to feel a little less judged."

This time they both know he's talking about Drew.

Incidentally, Drew is the only player who hasn't raced into the gym. He's taking his time, dragging his feet.

"I take it Drew's not playing again today?" Mac asks.

He starts to say that he gets to decide who plays and

who doesn't, but then nods. "Borders is going to sit this one out."

"Missing your best shooter is going to make it a lot harder to win today," Mac says.

"Yes, it is," Coach agrees.

"You're going to get blamed if you lose."

"Yes I am."

And that's exactly what happens.

Drew sits on the bench quietly, Larry stands and shouts, and the Predators lose badly.

The highlight of the game, as far as Mac's concerned, is when Larry leaves at the end of the first half.

The lowlight is when a few other parents leave with him.

Maybe they're not actually leaving *with* him. Maybe they just happen to be leaving at the same time.

But Larry is definitely talking at them as they leave, complaining about Coach Miller and his lack of a game plan that makes any sense.

And it looks to Mac as though they're listening.

PREDATORS BECOME PREY, NO LONGER IN FIRST PLACE

by Mac McKenzie

They went, they played, they were conquered. Coyote Canyon's boy's basketball team never quite looked like themselves today. Maybe it was poor Xs and Os. Maybe it was that indefinable quality called *intangibles* or a *lack of grit*. Maybe it was all of the above.

Their stats were indeed grim. Middlefield outrebounded the Predators, 31–17. They had 18 steals that turned into 28 fast break points. They shot significantly better from the field: 48 percent to 37 percent. But diagnosing this loss is more complicated than a list of statistics. Poor numbers weren't the only symptom. The Predators also appeared one step slow getting around screens and getting loose balls. Their energy picked up in the second half and for the first time in a week they went on a run of their own. But it was much too little and way too late.

The final score: Middlefield 52, Coyote Canyon 39.

The Predators' ongoing slump has left them with the same record as Middlefield (8–4). While they're still tied for first place, Middlefield's victory gives the Lions the tie-breaker. The good news: the Predators get one more shot at Middlefield in a couple weeks, this one at home.

The bad news: Middlefield is currently on a winning streak, and the Predators have lost two in a row.

CHAPTER 8

For once, Mac doesn't wake up the baby. He typed up his game recap with steady restraint. Like the Predators, he seemed to be moving on autopilot and as though he'd given up.

There was nothing he could do, he told himself. If no one would go on the record to talk about Larry Borders and the impact this man was having on both his son's and the team's morale, he couldn't write about it. Mac was a beat reporter, not a columnist. His hands were tied.

No wonder the Predators showed so much restraint tonight.

Still, he feels bad about the recap. For the first time in his sports reporting career, he feels as though he just lied to his readers. He claimed in the article that there was no diagnosis for what ailed the Predators, when in fact he could pinpoint the very root cause of their shoddy play.

That's when his phone rings . . .

WAAAAAAAAAA!

. . . and wakes up the baby.

"I'm so sorry," Drew says.

"You've already said that," Mac says in a hushed voice.

He's using his shoulder to trap the phone to his ear. His hands, after all, are occupied. He is holding Nora while attempting to steer and propel his chair. Mostly he is just rocking back and forth.

She's still making fussy noises, but her cries have finally become more like babbles. Her eyelids seem to be getting heavier too. The key is to keep moving and to keep his voice hushed.

"Do you want to tell me why you're calling?" Mac half-whispers.

There's a pause.

"Because my dad is taking me off the team."

"Really?" This is all Mac can think to say. He's surprised to hear this; it seems out of character for Larry Borders to give in or give up—or to let his son do these things. But what's even more surprising is the disappointment in Drew's voice. "Isn't this what you wanted? To be able to quit the team?"

"Not like this," Drew says. "My dad isn't letting me quit. He's starting his own team and making me play on it."

"Can he do that?"

"Apparently. Dad found some legal loophole or

something. We're going to be an independent team that plays all the same teams Coyote Canyon plays. He's already got a few games scheduled."

Mac's getting a crick in his neck so, in one move, he takes his hand off the wheel and switches the phone to the other shoulder.

"Where is he getting the players?" he asks.

"He's poaching them from Coyote Canyon. That's why I'm calling. He's already convinced a few parents to take their kid off the team and he's working on some more. He spent the last few hours calling them and making his case."

"Well, why are you telling me about it?" Mac says. Suddenly, he knows why Drew is calling him. He becomes angry.

"I didn't know who else to turn to," Drew says.

"How about your dad? Turn to him. Tell him you don't want to play on his team."

"I tried," Drew says. "He said I was selling myself short, whatever that means. Then he told me not to worry—it was all going to work out. It was pretty clear that that was the end of the discussion."

Only because you let it be, Mac thinks. But he knows he's being a little unfair. He's lucky to have parents who are supportive without being overbearing—who trust him to make good decisions and don't try to run his life. So he doesn't really know what it would be like to have a parent like Larry Borders.

The truth is that Mac wants to help. He realizes he's not upset about being dragged into this situation. What he's upset about is the fact that he can't do anything about it.

"Are you willing to be quoted in an article?" he asks Drew.

"Absolutely," Drew says. "Just so long as you don't use my name."

"We've been over this," Mac says. "*The Coyote Courier* doesn't use anonymous sources. We have high standards."

"And there's no way you can lower them?" Drew asks.

Mac is genuinely insulted. Is Drew seriously asking him to lower the paper's journalistic standards? While it's true that many of the most prestigious papers in the country sometimes use anonymous sources, they only do that when the source would literally lose their job if discovered. *The Coyote Courier* can't simply loosen its policies because an athlete won't talk to his dad, no matter how intimidating he is.

"I'm not just writing blog pieces," Mac says. "You know that, right? I'm writing actual articles for an actual paper."

"Could you?" Drew asks.

"Could I what?"

"Write about this in your blog instead?" Drew asks. "If you did that, could you use anonymous sources?"

For some reason, this had never occurred to Mac. He'd always used his blog for player profiles, scouting previews, or general thoughts about things he liked and disliked about a particular sport. Actual sports reports, though? Ones that included interviews to go along with his opinions? Maybe he should give it a try. It would mean he could finally, at long last, tell the whole truth.

"I'll think about it," Mac says.

But he already knows he's going to do it.

It's only after he's ended the call that he realizes Nora is sound asleep. All this time he'd assumed that noise—any noise—was what kept her awake. But apparently not. For some reason his voice didn't prevent her from nodding off again. Maybe she's entered a new phase? Maybe she's not so sensitive to sounds anymore. He sets her in her crib, makes sure it's secure, and goes back into the living room. He pries open his laptop. There's nothing to stop him from typing up a blog piece right now.

WAAAAAAAAA!

Okay, maybe Nora's not in a new phase after all.

He can start the blog piece tomorrow instead.

THE MAC REPORT
SPECIAL REPORT: SIDELINE PRESSURE

I'd like to take a break from my usual blog content to examine an important issue—and threat—facing the Predators' boys' basketball team.

Anyone who has attended a recent Coyote Canyon boys' basketball game knows who Larry Borders is. Anyone who hasn't *should* know who he is. Mr. Borders is, by all accounts, a high-powered attorney. He's also, as far as I'm concerned, a pain in the neck.

And that's being kind.

Mr. Borders spends entire games stalking the sidelines, pacing back and forth endlessly. The only thing that moves more than his feet are his lips. The man won't shut up. One can only assume he shows more restraint in the courtroom—otherwise, the judge would be at risk of developing tennis elbow from over-striking his gavel.

Admittedly, if Mr. Borders were just a loudmouth, he'd be committing no crime. His tirades would be out of bounds at a middle school basketball game but not out of order in a courtroom. Unfortunately, he is doing more than talking these days.

According to a source that wishes to remain

anonymous, his son, sick of being yelled at by his own father, begged his coach to bench him.

The same source reports that Mr. Borders has decided to pull his son from the program altogether and start his own team. Three guesses as to who will be the coach.

That's not all. The same source says that Mr. Borders has been actively recruiting other players from the Coyote Canyon squad.

Unlike Mr. Borders, I'm no lawyer. I don't know if any of the above actions are illegal. I do know they're more than a little sinister.

That's why I've decided to write about them in this blog.

While I may not have a case in the court of law against Mr. Borders, I'm hoping I have a case in the court of public opinion.

So far, parents have failed to put a stop to Mr. Borders' behavior. Some, my source informs me, have made verbal agreements to remove their sons from the Predators and put them on Mr. Borders' new team.

If our parents won't stand up for the school's program, maybe the students will instead.

CHAPTER 9

"Can you publish this?" Samira asks. "About a parent?"

"I don't know," Mac admits.

They're at his house, in the living room, sitting on the couch with his laptop between them. They're the only ones there. Mac's older sister and dad are gone for another week visiting more colleges. His baby sister's in day care. His mom's at work. Samira stopped by after school to read over what he'd written. Luckily, it was a slow sports day at school, so Mac doesn't feel too guilty about taking a day off his reporting duties.

There's a replay of a college basketball game on TV, muted.

"You don't hold back," Samira says.

"I was sick of holding back."

Samira's looking at the computer screen, rereading. "I like it," she finally concludes.

"Thanks. But should I publish it?"

Samira shrugs. "Have you shown it to Drew?"

"I wrote it during study hall and emailed him a copy.

I told him I completely understood if it was too critical of his dad and he didn't want me to publish it."

"Did he email back?" Samira asks.

"Within half an hour," Mac says. "Just three words: *Go for it.*"

"Well then, maybe you should."

"Maybe."

"Want me to come up with some figures showing the Predators' decline over the last week? Maybe we could do a plus-minus on Mr. Borders. Whenever he's there, here's how bad the team plays; whenever he's gone, here's how well they play. That sort of thing."

"Maybe next time," Mac says.

"So there's going to be a next time?"

Mac shrugs.

"Because if there's a next time," Samira points out, "there must be a first time."

They look at the computer screen some more.

"Oh, what the heck," Mac says, clicking the button to post it to his blog. "No one will probably read it anyway."

"I wouldn't be so sure," Samira says.

She grabs the remote and turns on the volume.

The next day at school, Mac does his best to forget about the blog post, but it isn't easy. He doesn't know what, exactly, he's expecting people to say or do—but he's expecting them to say or do *something*.

After all, he's taken a real risk. While there is a part of him that hopes no one will read the blog post, the rest of him *needs* them to read it. Maybe that's why he's never kept a diary or journal. He's never seen the point of writing something if no one else is going to read it.

Besides, he cares about sports at Coyote Canyon, and

not just because it's his job to care. He isn't just a reporter; he's a fan. The main purpose of writing the blog post is to save the Predators basketball team from Drew's dad.

If no one reads the post, and no one hears about Larry Borders' plan to take players from the Predators, their season is in serious trouble.

That's why Mac sits in class and waits for someone to look at their phone (even though they're not supposed to) and read his blog. He eats lunch with Samira and they both expect the cafeteria to start buzzing with the scandal Drew has exposed. He moves through the halls and wonders when he'll hear other students say, "Did you hear about Drew's dad?"

But none of this happens.

Mac is trying to convince himself that this is for the best—maybe there's another way to save the Predators, a way that's less risky for him personally—when he gets to the bullpen at the end of the day. He turns on the computer at his desk and goes to his blog. Scrolling down, he sees that someone has commented on his post.

"This is Larry Borders," the comment says. "Please be aware that this post defames my character. If it is not removed by the end of the day, I will be filing a lawsuit against you."

CHAPTER 10

"Sorry."

Mac whips his head around, startled.

"Drew," he says. "You've got to stop just showing up like that."

Drew's in his school clothes, holding a paper grocery bag—which seems strange, obviously, but Mac doesn't have time to worry about that right now.

"Sorry," Drew says again.

Mac takes a deep breath. "It's fine. You didn't mean to scare me. I was just—your dad, he says he's suing me."

"I know. That's actually why I was saying sorry." Drew's entire body is slumped against the doorframe. It's as if his shoulder is fastened to it, keeping him from sliding right to the floor. "I screwed everything up. I couldn't talk to my own father so I made you write a blog that only made everything worse."

Looking at Drew like that makes Mac angry. He knows Drew's being honest—that he really does feel badly. But what Mac needs right now isn't sympathy or an apology. What he needs is a good lawyer. Drew obviously can't give him that—but he can at least stand up straight and not look like all hope is lost.

"How did he see the post?" Mac asks.

"I showed it to him."

No wonder he's slumping.

"I made sure to read it this morning while eating breakfast," Drew continues, "and then I said something like, 'Uh-oh.' He asked me what the matter was, and I showed him your post. I knew he wouldn't take it well, but I didn't think he'd sue you."

"Can he sue me?" Mac asks. "Legally, I mean? Did I do anything illegal?"

"I don't know."

Mac thinks about this. For some reason, he doesn't feel afraid or defeated. Maybe it's because Drew already feels enough of those things for both of them. He once heard someone say that: there can only be 100 percent of any emotion. If someone is freaking out over something, the other person is usually much calmer. "Know any lawyers besides your dad?"

"What I know is that my dad almost never loses," Drew says. "My advice? Take the post down as soon as possible."

"And then what?" Mac asks.

"Avoid getting sued."

"Yeah, but what happens to you? What happens to the team?"

Drew tilts the paper bag he's holding so Mac can see the Coyote Canyon basketball jersey and shorts inside. "I'm going to turn these in right now."

"What about the other players?" Mac asks. "Are they switching teams too?"

"I don't know. Dad must have talked with all the parents by now, but he didn't tell me who's leaving the Predators. Where are you going?"

Mac has already started for the door. "To do my job."

He stops several feet from the door. Slouched like that, Drew is blocking Mac's way out.

"Don't you want to take the blog post down first?" Drew asks.

"Your dad said I have until the end of the day to remove it."

"Why not just take it down now?"

"I'm a reporter," Mac says. "I don't like to quit a story before it's finished."

It looks as though Drew is going to say something else, so Mac starts wheeling toward him—fast. He's so sick of seeing Drew slouch, he'll ram right into him if he needs to. Anything to snap Drew out of his stupor.

At the last second, Drew straightens himself and makes room for Mac to charge through the door and down the hallway.

By the time Mac nears the gym, he's practically zooming down the halls. He has a lot of players to interview, and he doesn't have a lot of time to do it. It occurs to him that "the end of the day" might mean the end of the business day—which is, what, 5:00?

That would mean he has less than two hours to do his interviews and learn anything useful from the players.

This thought doesn't discourage him; it gets him more riled up, in a good way. He's determined to get what he needs.

The truth is that he doesn't have any idea himself what he needs (other than a good lawyer). Nor does he know what he's going to do with the information he gets from the players.

Drew had asked him why he didn't remove the story right away, and it's totally possible he's just being stubborn. Likely, even. He's never liked people telling him what to do. One of the reasons he became a reporter was so that he could decide which sport to cover and which story to tell. The only person who gets to tell him what he can and can't write is his editor.

Which isn't really true—he gets that. In less than two hours he'll probably need to take the blog post down. A single sports story isn't worth getting sued over.

What he's doing now, racing to the gym, is a mostly pointless act of defiance. But it feels good to do it anyway.

He pushes the doors to the gymnasium open, contemplating whom he should talk to first.

Except it isn't a question. There's only one player there.

Diego.

Mac looks at the clock on the wall. It's 3:28. Practice should have started by now, right?

"Are you the first one here?" Mac asks. Like last time, he plants himself under the basket Diego's shooting at.

"First and last," Diego says. He's at the free-throw line. After two dribbles, he takes a shot. It rattles around the rim, then settles in and through the net. "Practice was cancelled."

"On account of what?" Mac says, catching the basket-ball and passing it back to Diego.

"On account of almost everyone quitting."

Mac's heart sinks. *I'm too late*, he realizes.

He takes another two dribbles, another shot. It rims out.

"Almost everyone?" Mac asks, gliding to the bouncing ball. He's not sure why he's still here—the mission to save the team has clearly failed. Then again, he's a reporter and there are still plenty of questions he doesn't yet have answers to.

"Four of five starters, at least three others."

"Did they say why?" Mac throws Diego a bounce pass.

"Drew's dad is starting a new team," Diego answers.

"I heard about that."

"He promised to start the ones who aren't starting for the Predators. He promised everyone more playing time and more chances to shoot."

Another shot, another miss. It's not like Diego to miss two free throws in a row. He's usually a machine at the line. Mac wonders if he's more rattled than he's pretending to be.

"Did Drew's dad recruit you too?" Mac asks.

"Yep." Diego responds without taking his eyes off the rim.

"Why'd you say no?"

Diego stops shooting the ball. He holds it against his hip and looks directly at Mac.

"Two reasons," he says.

"The first?"

"I don't appreciate Mr. Borders reaching out to my parents instead of me. Especially if he's going to lie to them."

"Lie to them?"

Diego nods. "He said that Coach Miller didn't know anything about basketball and that if he did, I'd be a star by now."

"I bet your parents liked hearing that," Mac says.

Another nod. "Too bad it's not true. I've been thinking about and practicing and studying basketball non-stop for

MAC'S SPORTS REPORT

a couple years now, and Coach still helps me see things on the court that I would have never thought about."

Mac knows what he means. The few times he's gotten Coach to open up about Xs and Os, Mac has left the office smarter than he'd entered. The NBA commentator Mike Breen always talks about how former New York Knicks coach Jeff Van Gundy taught him almost everything he knows about basketball, and Mac has had similar experiences with Coach Miller.

"You don't think you could be a star?" Mac asks.

"I know I couldn't. Not yet, probably not ever. I get up

at four o'clock in the morning every day to come here—even weekends. Do you know who gets here early to unlock the gym?"

"Coach?" Mac guesses.

"Most mornings he even gives me a practice workout to follow," Diego adds.

This is the first time Mac has heard about the early morning workouts, probably because Coach didn't want him to know about it. Unlike Mr. Borders, Coach Miller would rather spotlight his players than himself.

"Think about that. He gets up early every morning to work with a kid who isn't good enough to start."

"You have gotten pretty good, Diego," Mac says. "You're a key player on a good team."

Diego continues as if Mac hasn't spoken. "In other words, I'm a role player. Which is fine. I do think I'm getting pretty good. I'm just saying that however good I am, it's because of Coach, not in spite of him."

He takes another two dribbles, bends his knees, shoots. Swish.

"Didn't you say there's two reasons why you didn't quit the team?" Mac asks.

"Math," Diego says, his eyes still on the rim.

"Math?"

"He told at least eight players' parents that their son would be a starter. Unless he's planning to start an 8-on-8 league, Mr. Borders is lying.

He shoots another free throw. That one goes in too.

Mac rebounds the ball, passes it to Diego, then backs away for the doors.

"Hey, Diego," he says.

"Yeah?"

"Was this on the record or off?"

"You can quote every word, man."

CHAPTER 11

It's now 4:39 p.m. and Mac has to make a decision.

He's back in the bullpen, staring at his computer screen.

Should he remove his first blog post? Or should he publish his *next* blog post?

The first option is safer and probably smarter.

The second one is reckless and maybe even stupid.

But it's also bold.

And it sticks up for Drew, even if he won't stick up for himself. And for Diego, who deserves every second of playing time he's ever gotten. And even for Coach, who's never asked anyone to stick up for him, which just makes Mac respect him that much more.

The second option sticks up for the truth.

And isn't that what journalists are supposed to pursue no matter what?

Honestly, Mac's not sure why he spent so long thinking about his options—not when he knew all along what he was going to do.

He clicks on the button that publishes his latest blog post.

THE MAC REPORT
SPECIAL REPORT:
SIDELINE PRESSURE, GUT CHECK

Yesterday I posted a story about Larry Borders, the father of a Coyote Canyon Middle School basketball player. I didn't pull any punches. Mr. Borders has spent the last several games yelling at his son and the coach, and I said as much.

Using a source that wished to remain anonymous, I reported that Mr. Borders' son, Drew, was so embarrassed by his father's antics, he asked to be benched. The same source indicated that Mr. Borders was calling players' parents and trying to poach these players for a new team Mr. Borders plans to coach.

The result of this reporting was a legal threat from Mr. Borders himself. He claimed he was planning to sue me for defamation of character if I didn't remove my first post.

As I said last time, I'm no lawyer. I don't know whether I've in some way broken the law, but I doubt it. After all, to the best of my knowledge, every word of my post is the truth.

So rather than remove my post, I've decided to invite

Mr. Borders to reread it. If I have gotten any of the facts wrong, please, Mr. Borders, let me know. I'd be happy to take those down. I also invite any of the players or their parents to contact me and let me know if I've unfairly represented Mr. Borders' attempts to take players from the Coyote Canyon squad.

So far, all the evidence I've seen confirms my initial reporting. I attended the boys' basketball practice today, but found myself one of only two people in the gym.

The other person was Diego Lunez, a key player off the bench for the Predators. I asked him where the rest of the Coyote Canyon team was, and he informed me that many of them had quit in order to join Mr. Borders' team.

Mr. Borders, Diego claimed, promised each of these players they would start on his new team.

In fact, Diego said, he made the same promise to Diego's parents.

Putting eight starters on the court is, as Diego pointed out, a mathematical impossibility.

Diego also took issue with the way Mr. Borders insulted Coach Miller's coaching ability. He told me that Coach Miller works with him on his game every morning, even during the weekend, and that he "helps me see things on the court that I would have never thought about."

Again, if anyone—Mr. Borders or any of the parents or players—disputes any of my reporting, I welcome your corrections.

If no one does dispute these facts, then it is, to use a sports cliché, gut check time.

Who has the guts to admit they got conned? Who's willing to help me save the formerly proud Predators' boys' basketball team?

This time, Mac has decided, publishing a blog post isn't enough.

He needs to advertise it.

The first people he texts a link to of the new blog post are Samira and Ty. Both agree to share it with as many people as possible. Samira says they should come up with a way to track who gets the most people to open the link. Ty says, "Mac, you write like an old man. No offense. You sound like a real sports writer. It's awesome. Dorky, but awesome."

From there, Mac spends the rest of the night at home, on social media, texting, emailing—asking everyone he knows to spread the word about his blog on their own social media pages.

"Everything going okay?"

It's his mom. She picks a stuffed animal off the floor and tosses it into a teetering basket in the corner.

"I'm not sure," Mac says honestly.

"Anything I can help with?"

"Same answer."

"When you are sure, let me know, okay?" his mom says. "It's kind of my job to help."

Mac watches her scoop up a rubber duck and flip it at the basket. She's got good aim—the duck lands on the pile of toys—but it bounces off and skitters to the floor. To his surprise, his mom doesn't cross the room to pick up the toy. She cares about neatness more than anyone else he knows; for her to leave the toy on the floor means she must be really tired. Between taking care of the baby on her own these last couple weeks and working long shifts at the ER, sleep has been hard to come by.

"You're not at your job," Mac reminds her.

"Being a mom is a job too," she says. "A great job, but a job."

He knows she means it—that he could tell her

anything—but he doesn't see the point right now. He'd rather she got some much-needed sleep.

He tells her goodnight and gets back to his emailing.

As usual, the more passionate his writing becomes, the louder he types.

WAAAAAAAA!

If only baby Nora knew English. With her lung power, he wouldn't even need social media. He could just have her wail out the information about Larry Borders and the whole school district would probably hear it.

This time Mac doesn't have to wait until the next day to find out if anyone read his blog post. He already has hundreds of likes and dozens of shares by the time he gets Nora to sleep and checks his phone. There are also tons of comments like "you are awesome" and "great blog" and "dope!"

It's good to get the encouragement, but what matters more are the longer messages. He wakes up early the next morning and finds several.

They're from players and their parents.

"He told me Coach Miller was playing favorites," one parent says.

"Thanks to Larry," another parent writes, "I was under the impression that one of the starters was getting so much court time because he's related to Coach Miller. After reading your reports, I asked my son and he said he didn't think anyone on the team was related to Coach. Did Larry just make that up? Who would do that?"

"Have you interviewed Coach at all?" one player asks. "How mad is he? Do you think he'll let me back on the team?"

That last one is a common refrain: *Will Coach let me rejoin?*

It occurs to Mac that he hasn't talked with Coach Miller in a few days—not since he was kicked out of his office last week.

Will he let players back on the team?

How does he feel about the way Mac has made this situation public?

These are good questions.

And Mac decides that now is as good a time as any to ask them.

Especially since, thanks to Diego, Mac is pretty sure where to find Coach.

CHAPTER 12

Mac's mom drops him off at school a little after five o'clock the next morning. Diego hasn't arrived yet, but sure enough, he finds Coach Miller unlocking the gym doors.

"Coach?" Mac asks. "Wondering if I can bother you with a few questions."

"You can ask them," Coach says. "I can't promise that you'll bother me with them."

Coach Miller walks toward the corner of the gym, unlocks the supply closet and then disappears into it. A few seconds later, a basketball comes rolling out.

Mac scoops it up as Coach emerges.

"You shoot," Coach says. "I'll rebound."

Like any good shooter, Mac starts close to the basket. That way he can concentrate on his release without having to use other muscles to get the ball to the rim. Just as importantly, he can watch the ball go in over and over and over. It's a psychological thing. At some point, he'll begin scooting his chair farther from the rim—but only once he's gotten used to making every shot he takes.

For a while Mac shoots in silence and Coach rebounds for him. Then Mac remembers why he came here.

"Do you know about the special series on my blog I started this week?" he asks Coach Miller.

"Drew mentioned them yesterday when he tried to hand in his uniform," Coach says.

"Tried?"

"I told him the same thing I wish I'd told all those other players yesterday. Keep the uniform in case you change your mind. I was too caught off guard to say it to most of them at the time." He watches Mac make another shot. "That's a nice follow through."

"Oh. Thanks." The truth is that Mac is doing the same shooting routine he's had for years; it's all muscle memory at this point. He hardly even realizes he's shooting. "According to some messages I got this morning, I think some of the players will take you up on your offer. Want me to tell them that?"

Coach catches the ball out of the net and stares at it, considering Mac's offer. "No. Let them step up and talk to me on their own. It'll be good for them and the team. Sometimes over-helping can be a mistake."

"Then why did you help Drew? Why did you let his dad think you benched his son?"

"Maybe I shouldn't have," Coach admits. "But I looked at Drew and saw a kid who really needed help, who in this situation truly felt helpless. Also, I really don't like Larry Borders. That's probably not something I should admit to a kid your age, especially a sportswriter."

He flips Mac the basketball.

"I don't like him either," Mac says. "I probably shouldn't be admitting that as a reporter."

He shoots again, holding the follow through as the ball drops through the net with plenty of backspin.

"I read your blog posts," Coach says. "I'm biased, but they struck me as solid reporting. Still, remind me never to get on your bad side" Coach says cracking a smile.

Mac catches Coach's pass and a split second later the ball is up in the air again, arcing perfectly to the center of the hoop.

"Does that mean from now on you're going to answer all my questions in complete sentences?" Mac asks.

"Don't count on it."

"Fair enough. But how come? I mean, what's the point of constantly fending off my questions? If you had talked to me the other day, there's a chance we could have avoided what happened. If the other players' parents realized Drew's dad was so overbearing that his own son asked to sit on the bench, they might not have allowed him to talk them into leaving the team."

"Some things are between me and my team, McKenzie. Just because I didn't tell people doesn't mean I was hiding it. It just means it was none of their business. Does that make sense?"

"I think so," Mac says.

"Look at it this way. You're a star basketball player, McKenzie. I don't mean that hypothetically. I've watched you play. You're the best player on your team and probably in the whole league."

"You've watched me play?" Mac can't help feeling flattered.

"Are you kidding? I wish we could use you on our squad. You're the best shooter in the whole dang school."

"Thanks." Because praise makes Mac uncomfortable, he adds: "I see what you're doing. You're trying to flatter me into asking easy questions, is that it?"

It's a joke, and Coach gets it. He smiles and passes Mac the ball.

"So here's my question for you," Coach says. "Why did you just do that? Why did you try to change the subject? Why don't you ever offer shooting tips to my players, or mention your own athletic feats in your writing?"

Mac takes a second to consider this. "I'm a reporter," he finally says. "It's my job to make my stories about the athletes and the games they play—not about me."

"Exactly," Coach says. "And I'm a coach—which means it's my job to do the same thing. This isn't about me. It's about them."

Mac keeps shooting and Coach keeps rebounding until the door opens and Diego walks in.

"I've got a new workout for you, Lunez," Coach says. He pulls a folded piece of paper out of his pocket and turns to give it to Diego.

"I'm going to go," Mac says. "Am I correct in assuming that all of this was on the record?"

"If I see any of this make it to print, I'll be angry about it, McKenzie."

"Thought so," Mac says. "You can't blame me for trying."

"I don't."

"Oh, Coach—one more question. Is anyone on the team related to you?"

Coach gives a puzzled look. "Related? Not that I know of."

"I didn't think so. Thanks, Coach."

MAC'S SPORTS REPORT

Mac leaves the gym feeling pretty good about himself. For the first time ever, he's gotten Coach to truly open up, even if it was off the record.

He checks his phone and finds more good news. In the hour or so since he last looked, his blog has gotten dozens more hits and shares. He also received a few more written messages. Scanning through them, they all seem positive.

As he's reading through the messages, his phone vibrates. He doesn't recognize the number, so he lets it go to voicemail. Whoever it is, they leave a message. As he looks through his call history, it appears this number has left several voicemails.

Mac clicks on the first message.

"Stuart McKenzie, this is Larry Borders. I'm calling to tell you that this is your last warning. Delete your posts about me or I will not hesitate to sue you."

He listens to the next message—left minutes after the first—and it's another legal threat. The next message is even more threatening. There's legal jargon that Mac has never heard before.

It's chilling to be gliding through the near-empty halls of school, hearing that his life as he knows it might be just about over. Some kids like to compare school to being in prison, but now here he is, in school while being threatened with actual imprisonment.

Wait. Can you go to prison if you lose a lawsuit? Mac's not sure. What if you can't afford to pay? In school they learned about debtors' prison. Is that still a thing?

For all he knows, the answer to all the above is *yes*. In the very near future someone will lock him up and throw away the key.

Maybe.

But for whatever reason, Mac has trouble imagining that this is the end of his freedom.

He's scared—that goes without saying—but he's not as scared as he should be.

In fact, with every new message he listens to from Mr. Borders, something funny happens. His fear starts to disappear altogether.

He's listening to another message from Mr. Borders, this one telling him to "cease and desist his scurrilous actions," when the phone starts beeping.

Another call from the same number.

Mac takes the call.

"Mr. Borders," he says.

"Stuart McKenzie. This is your final—"

"Yeah, you've said that about ten times now," Mac

interrupts. "Which I'm assuming means it's an empty threat. Either way, I have a few questions and comments for you as well. Do *you* know that *I* know about even more of the lies you told parents and players? I won't go into the details but let's just say more sources are contacting me by the hour and they don't make you look very good. I'm ready and willing to publish them, especially if you do anything to carry out your legal threats. At that point, what would I have to lose? This is *your* final warning, Mr. Borders. And unlike you, I mean it."

He hangs up the phone. To his surprise, there's clapping. Several students have gathered in the hall.

"Nice!" one of them says.

"Sticking it to the man!" says another.

"Remind me never to get on your bad side!"

They clap their hands and clap his shoulders and he tells himself that there's nothing to worry about.

Mac wants to believe he's in the clear, and with all the adrenaline pumping through his body he sort of does. But there's also a part of him that's far less certain. He just chewed out a high-powered attorney who doesn't scare off easily if at all. This is a man whose loud mouth got him kicked out of a middle school basketball game. Rather than staying away from the next few games out of shame, he came back and yelled even louder.

Telling off loudmouth attorneys definitely feels good . . . right up until that loudmouth attorney sics the police on you.

CHAPTER 13

There's still time before class starts, and Mac needs to clear his head. He finds the gym empty and cuts across the gleaming hardwood floor to the supply closet. The door is closed but he tries the handle anyway. It turns. The room isn't very big but it's dark. The air is thick with the stench of rarely washed pinnies. Once his eyes adjust he spots the bag of basketballs and takes one.

While talking with Coach Miller this morning he didn't get to finish his shooting drills, so that's what he'll do now.

He stations himself about twelve feet from the basket and makes several shots in a row. Then he moves to another spot, still twelve feet from the hoop. He's trying to get in a shooting zone—the kind of zone that requires his full focus and that blocks out everything else.

He tells himself to concentrate—on the rim, on the dimples on the basketball, on the imaginary shot clock in his head. He's always been a good late-game shooter, and he thinks it's because he's been imagining taking last-second shots for as long as he can remember.

"Hey!"

Snapped out of his zone, Mac spins around

"You've GOT to stop sneaking up on me like that," Mac says.

"Sorry. It's just . . . I got here a few minutes ago and you haven't missed a single shot," Drew says.

"I try not to."

"Me neither. It just doesn't always work. Why didn't I know you were a great shooter?"

"I've never told you," Mac says.

"Why not? Is it like your secret identity or something? Your superpower is that you never miss a shot?"

Drew is now standing right next to Mac. He doesn't need to yell. But he's so excited about his new discovery that he can't help raising his voice.

"It's not a secret," Mac tells him. "I just keep my playing career separate from my reporting career."

"Career?" Drew looks surprised. "Are you saying you play in a league? When's your next game?"

"Tomorrow, actually," Mac says.

"Can I come? I mean, are fans invited?"

Mac can't help laughing. "What league wouldn't want fans?"

"Good point." Drew looks a little sheepish.

"Your dad spent all morning telling me he's going to press charges," Mac says.

"Do you believe him?"

Mac gave a little shrug. "I told him I didn't, but . . . do *you* believe him? You know him better than I do."

"I'm starting to think I don't know him as well as I thought I did. Ever since the divorce, it's like he's out to prove something. Mom left him and . . . ."

Drew's voice trails off. There's a long, awkward silence.

"What are you doing here?" Mac says, trying to change the subject. "I thought you had given up on basketball . . ."

"I guess I thought coming here would help me remember what I used to like about it."

Mac offers him the basketball. "Maybe shooting will jog your memory."

"Are you kidding?" Drew asks. "There's no way I'm shooting *now*. Not after that shooting clinic you just put on. I'd be way too self-conscious every time I missed. You know, up until this moment, I considered myself a good shooter, but now?"

"Sorry?" Mac isn't sure what Drew is talking about.

"Yeah. You should apologize. If there's one person who owes the other an apology, it's clearly you," Drew says good-naturedly.

They both laugh because the truth is obviously the other way around.

Mac thinks about asking Drew one more time to confront his father. But, really, what would that accomplish? By now, Larry Borders is on a mission. It's hard to believe anyone could stop him, not even his son. Mr. Borders is furious because Mac described how he was behaving and he didn't like what that reality looked like. There's probably no reasoning with a man like that.

"What are you going to do?" Drew asks.

"What else is there to do? Try not to think about it and keep living my life. I hope my game tomorrow will help distract me."

By the time Samira's dad brings Mac home, his mom is already asleep. The girls' basketball game went into overtime, and Samira didn't call her dad to pick them up until after she'd crunched some numbers from her scorebook. Mac wonders if he should wake his mom. At some point, he should probably tell her that a lawyer may be in the process of suing her son.

He inches into her room and hears her heavy, peaceful breathing and he just can't wake her. She worked a double shift at the emergency room over the last twenty-four hours, then picked the baby up from day care in time to make dinner. Mac knows his mom well enough to expect that leftovers will be waiting for him in the fridge. She's earned this deep sleep, he decides. And really, what would waking her up so late at night accomplish? What could she or anyone else do to fix the problem at 10:30 p.m.? The good news is that, for once, there's no reason for him to type anything, which means there's no risk of waking his baby sister.

It's only a few moments after thinking this that his phone rings.

WAAAAAAAAAA!

He looks at his phone while hurrying into the baby's room.

It's Larry Borders' number.

No. Wait. It's not. It looks like his number, but is slightly different.

Nora's still crying as he scoops her up and answers the phone.

"Drew?" Mac says into the phone.

"He's coming to your game tomorrow."

"Who?" Mac asks.

"What do you mean *who*? My dad," Drew answers.

Nora continues to fuss but settles onto Mac's lap.

"You told him I play basketball?"

"No, I swear I didn't."

Mac maneuvers out of Nora's bedroom and into the living room. Even with all the lights off, Mac manages to avoid the loudest creaks on the wood floor.

"Then how . . . ?"

"I think he Googled you. Are there box scores and stuff of your games?"

He's never had to look up any box scores; Samira keeps track of the statistics, and hers are much more in-depth than a typical box score. But he's pretty sure the league posts online standings, rosters, and generic stats.

"What is he planning to do at the game?" Mac asks.

"I don't know. I told him not to go, but he blew me off."

Mac's impressed that Drew tried to keep his dad from going to the game.

"Honest question," Mac says. "Is he dangerous?"

"You mean, like, physically?"

"Yes," Mac says.

"No way. His mouth is what's dangerous. Especially when he's upset about something. And he's really upset with you."

"Is he coming in person to serve me some papers? Like, legal documents or something?"

Mac must not be paying close enough attention because he sideswipes the high chair, jostling the baby. She makes a few noises of complaint but settles back onto his lap.

"He didn't say," Drew answers, then pauses. "Are you still going to play in the game?"

"I have to. It's the last game of the regular season. If we win we are in the playoffs."

"Are you serious?" Drew sounds incredulous. "You're seriously thinking about the playoffs right now?"

"What else am I going to think about? Should I plan to live the rest of my life in hiding?"

Drew takes in a breath. "You know, you look like a regular person, Mac. But you don't act like one."

Since they're talking over the phone, Mac can't see Drew's facial expression. It's totally possible that he basically just called Mac weird—but Mac's pretty sure he meant it to be a compliment.

"Thanks?" Mac says.

There isn't much else to say—Mac's mind is clearly made up—so they hang up. The house is quiet. Too quiet, he now realizes. Nora stirs and Mac starts making the only noise he can think of: the Harlem Globetrotters theme song. Instantly, Nora's body goes limp and her breathing gets deeper.

Once Nora is safe and content in her crib, Mac pivots toward his own bedroom.

Something tells him it's going to be hard to get himself to fall asleep tonight.

CHAPTER 14

As Mac waits his turn in the layup line, he tries to get himself to focus—to get in the zone. He catches a pass and dribbles a few times and, for the first time in years, loses control of the ball off his chair.

"You okay, Mac?" Ty asks.

"Fine," Mac lies, retrieving the ball and going in for his layup.

A few minutes before the start of the game, Mac's team begins an open shootaround. Mac's first few shots clang off the rim, but it's not the fact that he missed that worries Mac. What worries him is that he can't seem to get out of his own head. Despite the thousands and thousands of shots Mac has taken in his life, today his form feels awkward, somehow different. He's second-guessing what has always been instinctual. *Do I always tilt my head back and watch the ball after it leaves my hands?* he wonders. *Or do I keep my eyes on the rim?*

Quit being so self-conscious, he tells himself.

But he can't help it. Every few minutes, he checks the crowd again to see if Larry Borders has arrived.

"Mac!"

It's Ty.

Mac swivels his head just in time to see the ball sailing quickly toward him. He doesn't have time to catch it; but he's able to get his hands up in time to block the basketball from hitting his face.

"Sorry, man," Ty says. "I called your name before I threw the pass; guess you didn't hear me."

It's right before the pre-game warm-up buzzer goes off that Larry Borders finally arrives. All this time, without even knowing it, Mac had created a mental video of Mr. Borders' arrival. In his mind, Mr. Borders would stroll in with slicked back hair and wearing an expensive suit plus dress shoes that glistened. Two other suited, hunched-over men would shuffle behind him, lugging a black leather briefcase.

In real life, none of this happens. There are no lackeys following close behind Mr. Borders. There is no suitcase. Mr. Borders isn't in a suit and his hair isn't slicked back. If anything, it's unkempt—maybe even unwashed. In fact, the man doesn't look like Mr. Borders, attorney-at-law; he just looks like Larry, unshaven and in a rumpled sweatshirt with a few paint specks on it. His eyes are either tired or wild or both.

A lot of people would probably think the real-life Larry is scarier than the Mr. Borders Mac had conjured.

But not Mac.

All Mac cares about is that there's no briefcase. If there's no briefcase, there are no legal documents. Besides, the guy who just arrived doesn't look ready to make a legal argument; he just looks like a guy who's ready to heckle.

Which doesn't faze Mac one bit.

The starters on each team roll out to the court and shake each other's hands.

For the first time in quite a while, Mac feels comfortable. He may not know the rules of law, but he knows the rules of basketball.

Right from the opening tip Mac is locked in. On defense, he bursts in front of a pass and takes off for the other end of the court. Usually he'd go all the way in for the layup. But Samira showed him a shot chart a few days ago breaking down the percentages and math of shooting a three versus shooting a layup—and it turns out that, over the long run, really good shooters are better off shooting threes.

Mac, of course, is exactly that.

He stops his chair on a dime at the top of the key and drains the shot.

"Classic," Larry bellows. "This kid plays like he writes. It's all about him, all the time. He could do his job and take the easy layup, but then he wouldn't stand out from the crowd."

The smattering of fans in the stands turn to look at Larry, confused. *Who is this guy?* they seem to be asking.

Mac's teammates give him reassuring pats on the shoulder as they all get back to play defense.

Mac, of course, is glad to have such great teammates. But they don't need to worry about him. He feels great. He feels unstoppable. He feels, yes, in a zone. In THE zone—the one only really good players ever experience, and even for them it's rare. The game has slowed down for him. Everybody else appears to have brakes clamped onto their wheels. He feels as though he could dribble circles around them.

Out of the corner of his eye, Mac sees one of his opponents launch a ten-foot shot. As soon as it leaves the player's hand, Mac knows exactly where it will hit the rim and where it will bounce. He sees that Ty will be camped right under it so he takes off down the court while everyone else is still watching the shot. By the time Ty corrals the rebound and looks up the court, Mac is all alone on the other end. Ty heaves a football-style bomb the length of

the court, hitting Mac in a perfect position to catch the ball and lay it in.

"This kid," Larry bellows, shaking his head. "He leaks out early, completely deserting his team, failing to box out the guy he's supposed to be guarding, all in the off chance that he can score an easy bucket and add to his own point total."

Now heads are doing more than turning. They're scowling.

"Take it easy," someone says.

"No, I'm not going to take it easy," Larry says. "You should take it hard. If you let people get away with this me, me, me stuff, they'll never learn. They'll never treat others fairly."

"Whoa. Alright, buddy," the same guy who told Larry to take it easy says. "We're just trying to watch a game here."

Mac is too focused to pay attention to the conversation going on in the stands. A few minutes later, when his team is on offense again, he races across the baseline and catches a pass for a corner three. The other team has switched everything, so one of their long-armed post players comes charging at him, arm extended. Mac pump fakes, causing the post player's chair to go off-kilter. The post player tries to recover enough to avoid crashing into Mac, and almost succeeds but not quite. As the chairs glance off each other, Mac keeps his eyes up and his head stable. He launches a three with the defender practically falling in his lap. He doesn't see the trajectory of the basketball—the defender blocks his view—but the crowd lets him know it went in.

There's a whistle and a foul called. Mac helps the defender get situated back in his chair and makes his way to the free-throw line for a potential four-point play.

"Isn't that supposed to be an offensive foul now?" Larry Borders says. "Didn't they change the rule about offensive player leaning into a defensive player to draw the foul? Do rules even matter anymore?"

"That's enough."

This time, it isn't the guy in front of Larry who does the talking. It's someone from the other end of the bleachers.

"*Dad*—stop it."

It's Drew.

"Just knock it off," he says. "Can you hear yourself? Can you hear how you sound?"

He's making his way through the crowd.

"Drew, I know what I'm doing. *Somebody* has to—"

But Drew interrupts him: "If you can't hear yourself, then hear me. I'm the one who told Mac about your plan.

I'm the cowardly anonymous source you keep complaining about at home."

"You?" Larry says. They're next to each other on the bleachers. Larry stands up. He's clearly surprised. And furious. With them both standing, Larry is a good half foot taller than his son, and it looks as though he might spit on him or even, despite Drew saying his father wasn't violent, take a swing at him. His body is tense, his facial features rigid. Larry lifts a hand, ever so slightly.

His body goes from tense to loose in the blink of an eye. The blood drains from his cheeks.

"Why would you do that, Son?" he asks.

"I couldn't play in front of you anymore, Dad. I definitely couldn't play *for* you."

It's as if Larry's body has no bones in it anymore. The air coming out of Drew's mouth as he talks is almost enough to knock his father over.

"I was keeping you accountable," Larry says. "I needed you. I needed you to do your part so we could do this together. This was about both of us. I thought you saw that. It was about our family."

"I know you think that, Dad. But it wasn't about us—not to me. And if it wasn't about us, then it was just about you."

"Aren't you tired of everyone walking all over us?" Larry says.

"That's what you think happened. It's not what I think happened." Drew gestures to the court. "And it's definitely not what's happening right now. You're the one trying to walk over people, Dad. I understand if you can't see that right now. But I need you to take my word for it, okay?" When his dad doesn't say anything, he says more forcefully: "Okay?"

Drew's dad still doesn't respond—not in words. What he does is slump into Drew's arms.

There's silence because no one could possibly have anything to say after this intimate moment.

Nobody . . . except for Samira.

"And your opinions about basketball are a little outdated," she says.

"Are you kidding me right now, Samira?"

It's Ty, yelling at her from the court.

"What?" Samira says. "I'm just saying that your ideas about basketball were common a couple years ago until we developed a bunch of new statistics and metrics that proved the old ideas wrong."

Now there's definitely no one who knows what to say.

"Here," Samira says. She's holding a clipboard with a

bunch of charts and she pulls one out and folds it. "Let me know if you ever want to talk about the conclusions we can draw from this chart."

Mr. Borders appears to be in a daze, so Samira pressed the folded chart into his hand and closes his fingers around it.

After a few more awkward moments of no one talking, one of the referees blows her whistle to resume the game.

Ty rolls over to Mac, who's still standing at the free-throw line.

"You realize you caused all of this?" Ty says to Mac. "Aren't reporters supposed to make themselves invisible or something?"

He claps Mac's shoulder, shakes his head, laughs, and wheels away.

Mac misses the free throw and then watches chairs blur by him. He's pretty sure he's not in the zone anymore.

But that's okay. Having things go back to normal is fine by him.

CHAPTER 15

The next day, Coyote Canyon boys' basketball team has a game against Forrest View.

Mac's in his usual spot in the corner when Mr. Borders arrives. He looks at Mac with pursed lips and nods. Mac isn't sure how to read the expression. Is Mr. Borders nodding to acknowledge his leading role in the drama over the last few weeks? Or is he nodding the way people do when they're considering saying something maybe they shouldn't? Are his lips shut because he can't think of what to say or because he's trying to hold back from saying something?

Just to be safe, Mac returns his nod and doesn't say anything either. Drew has assured Mac that his father won't be filing a lawsuit. Still, Mac is in no hurry to provoke him.

Mr. Borders walks to his usual spot on the bleachers and sits down.

If he stays seated, Mac thinks, *maybe everything will be okay.*

But he doesn't stay seated. Mac has flashbacks of him pacing the sidelines, yelling at and across the court.

But this time Mr. Borders isn't looking at the court. He's scanning the bleachers. His eyes start in the corner where Mac is, and sweep slowly across the rest of the gym. Finally, they stop in the opposite corner, where Samira is sitting, scorebook ready. Mr. Borders makes his way toward Samira. There's an empty seat next to her, and he takes it. Then he reaches into his pocket, pulls out and unfolds the chart she gave him.

They're too far away; Mac can't hear what they're saying. But he can see that they're taking turns talking as they look at the chart. Mr. Borders shakes his head at one point while Samira's nodding hers—but if they disagree with each other, neither seems to mind.

Mac looks over to the bench. Drew is standing and stretching while he watches his father. He's smiling, something Mac suddenly realizes he hasn't seen him do in a long time. He's back in the starting lineup, and if he shoots anything in the game like he did in warm ups, he'll be one of the keys to a Predator win.

THE MAC REPORT
SPECIAL REPORT:
SIDELINE PRESSURE, FINAL SCORE

Over the last few days, I've used this blog to call attention to things going on off the basketball court.

And for good reason. I was doing my best to fend off a parent-led mutiny.

I'm happy to report that the mutiny has indeed been fended off.

That means I have a lot of people to thank.

Thank you to the players who were willing to talk, both anonymously and on the record. Thank you to the parents who reached out with more information. Thank you to everyone who read this blog in the effort to help save the Coyote Canyon boys' middle school basketball team.

Also, for concerned readers, Larry Borders and I talked yesterday. The lawsuit threatened against me did not have merit and was dropped. Our conversation was a great reminder for this reporter that sometimes it is easier to understand one another when you drop the pretense and talk one-on-one.

This is probably going to be my last special report

blog post for a while. I'm sick of reporting off-the-court drama, and will be happy to get back to player profiles, season highlights, and team previews next week.

Besides, the drama on the court is much more, well, dramatic.

Or at least it will be in a few days. Last night's game wasn't very dramatic at all. Now that the Predators team is intact again, they beat Forrest View with little difficulty.

Of course, it was just a warm up for their upcoming game against Middlefield. The rematch will be the last game of the regular season and a battle for first place.

As you no doubt remember, Middlefield turned our Predators into prey last time the two teams met. Still, there's reason for hope. Coyote Canyon looked like a brand-new team against Forrest View and the rematch will be a brand-new game.

I hope to see you there. If you can't make it, I'll do my best to capture the on-court action in my next game recap in *The Coyote Courier*.

PREDATORS AMBUSH MIDDLEFIELD, WIN CONFERENCE TITLE

by Mac McKenzie

If there was one word to describe what happened in the final game of the season between these two teams, it was *ambush*. Based on the team Middlefield saw only a couple weeks ago, it would have been nearly impossible for them to predict how quickly the Predators could pounce.

Both teams entered today's game with a record of 9–4, but Middlefield controlled its fate. By winning the first head-to-head matchup 52–39, they needed to either win today or to simply lose by less than 13 points.

Instead they got blown out by 36. And believe it or not, the final score, 64–28, is closer than the game felt.

The Predators combined ferocious team defense with rapid-fire passing and accurate shooting on the other end. Again and again, Middlefield's offense appeared mired in the mud. The ball would get stuck in the corner, where Coyote Canyon could trap and create turnovers. Those turnovers usually turned into Predator points. In all,

Coyote Canyon recorded 19 steals and only two turnovers themselves.

Despite having trouble putting in the gimmes of late, post Noah Crowder made all eight of his shots in the paint today and led the team in scoring with 21 points. The rest of the starters reached double digits as well. Off the bench, Diego Lunez contributed several quality minutes. According to the team statistician, in fact, Lunez had the highest plus-minus on the team (36). This game was billed to be a barn burner; instead, it was out of reach by the end of the half.

Coach Miller took his time taking each player out of the game for the last time. Each got his own standing ovation.

The ovation lasted until well after the buzzer sounded.

ABOUT THE AUTHOR

Paul Hoblin lives and teaches in St. Paul, Minnesota. He's written several other sports books, including *Foul*, which *Booklist* called "unbearably tense," and *Archenemy*, which won ALA's Rainbow Award.

ABOUT THE ILLUSTRATOR

Simon Rumble lives in the United Kingdom. He has worked as an illustrator in the creative industry, worldwide, for over twenty years.

MAC'S SPORTS REPORT

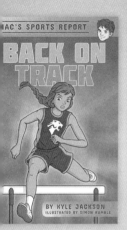

MAC'S SPORTS REPORT

BACK ON TRACK

BY KYLE JACKSON
ILLUSTRATED BY SIMON RUMBLE

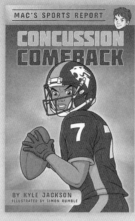

MAC'S SPORTS REPORT

CONCUSSION COMEBACK

7

BY KYLE JACKSON
ILLUSTRATED BY SIMON RUMBLE

MAC'S SPORTS REPORT

RACKET RUMORS

BY KYLE JACKSON
ILLUSTRATED BY SIMON RUMBLE

ALSO AVAILABLE

DON'T MISS MAC'S LATEST SPORTS SCOOPS

BY KYLE JACKSON
ILLUSTRATED BY SIMON RUMBLE

JOLLY FISH PRESS